A DILEMMA

Joris-Karl Huysmans by Félix Vallotton

A DILEMMA

JORIS-KARL HUYSMANS

TRANSLATED BY JUSTIN VICARI

WAKEFIELD PRESS, CAMBRIDGE, MASSACHUSETTS

Originally published as *Un dilemme*, 1888
This translation © 2015 Wakefield Press

Wakefield Press, P.O. Box 425645, Cambridge, MA 02142

This book was set in Garamond Premier Pro and Helvetica Neue Pro by Wakefield Press. Printed and bound by McNaughton & Gunn, Inc., in the United States of America. Interior photograph: Charles Marville, *Rue du Vieux Colombier, de la place Saint Sulpice*, ca. 1853–1870

ISBN: 978-1-939663-11-5

Available through D.A.P./Distributed Art Publishers
155 Sixth Avenue, 2nd Floor
New York, New York 10013
Tel: (212) 627-1999
Fax: (212) 627-9484

10   9   8   7   6   5   4   3   2   1

CONTENTS

TRANSLATOR'S INTRODUCTION

One of the most intriguing French writers of the nineteenth century, Joris-Karl Huysmans seemed to thrive on irascible contradictoriness. He was an uneasy disciple of the Naturalists and Émile Zola, sharing their avoidance of sentimentality, yet also resisting the yoking of fiction to narrow journalistic aims. He was the author of several books considered blasphemous in their time, yet he ended up as a convert to Roman Catholicism (and had displayed a tenacious interest in religiosity even when writing in defiance of it). He despised all things bourgeois, yet spent a good part of his life as an office bureaucrat, thus exposing himself almost daily to the bourgeoisie at its most pedantic, mendacious, and ill intentioned.

A Dilemma was Huysmans's most direct attack on bourgeois values. Though it was published in 1888, it was written and first serialized in 1884, almost directly after (and somewhat in reaction to) his preceding and best-known novel of that same year, *Against Nature*, and the ferocity of *A Dilemma*'s contempt for the bourgeoisie makes for something of a prequel to that previous book's account of a failed aristocratic quest for aesthetic spirituality. There has never been a precise equivalent in American English for everything that the "good bourgeois" represents (still) in French thought. We might be tempted to invoke this human embodiment of capitalism in the Babbits of Sinclair Lewis: narrow-minded small-town dwellers and such. But the French bourgeoisie were never restricted geographically (to the provinces or small towns) nor even socioeconomically (to the middle classes). In *A Dilemma*, Huysmans depicts what he called "the eternal turpitude of the bourgeois" as something that stretches from the urban slums of Paris to the regional farmlands, infecting the professional class (lawyers) but also the service class (concierges), and over at least two generations: specifically an old man, Le Ponsart, and his son-in-law, Lambois, both widowers whose only children have also died.

These chilly men are born provincials who had experience of city life in their youth, but are now retired gentlemen of leisure in the country. Trained in law, business, and politics, they are like an extremely malign version of Bouvard and Pécuchet, Flaubert's quixotic duo of naïfs: they know enough to make them dangerous, but not enough to make them kind. And they are about to go to war against a defenseless female, the pregnant mistress of Le Ponsart's deceased grandson, an attractive but undistinguished girl named Sophie, also of provincial stock and trying to make her way in Paris. Le Ponsart and Lambois are bent on cutting her out of the family estate.

The title's singular article, "A," turns out to be ironic: for Sophie the conflict has high stakes, whereas for the men it is simply another privilege to finesse, a legally framed "win-win" scenario

TRANSLATOR'S INTRODUCTION

that stands in stark contrast to the bald-faced "lose-lose" decision she is forced to make. In this sense, *A Dilemma* leverages a critique of nineteenth-century France that could apply in large part to our current age of Western neoliberalism, particularly in today's increasing state of crippled social mobility: the older generation has made its fortunes (largely through epic swindles), while the younger generation is stalled in economic stagnation. To be born poor, working-class, or lumpenproletariat is to be cursed to remain that way. The institutions of law, finance, and business (all characterized at different points in the novella) are ranked closely against the interests of those who need the most protection. It is possible, in this world as it is in ours today, to purchase such things as justice, virtue, and redemption; without the proper funding, however, such things are out of reach even to those who might naturally deserve them.

The bourgeois mentality, however, belies the all-consuming quicksand lying beneath it, and of which it is composed. The "dilemma" that this novella poses provides an inverted mirror to the one Des Esseintes ultimately faced in *Against Nature*: resign oneself to the mediocrity of a bourgeois existence in Paris and live, or follow the path of aristocratic aestheticism in the isolation of the countryside to insanity and death. The choice here is crueler, though: resign oneself to the working class in which you were born and eke out a marginal existence, or insist on your rights to a bourgeois existence and get thrown into the streets of Paris and starve.

Although the countryside is evoked as the place where the bourgeoisie go to settle down and live off their endowments, it is Paris where the harsh dog-eat-dog logic of bourgeois capitalism crystallizes. As it is in Huysmans's earlier novella, *Downstream*,

Paris is here a no-man's-land that belongs only to sharpies and crooks (and imagined sharpies and crooks): merchants struggle to stay afloat, clerks trundle to work in broken shoes. No one definitively owns this teeming metropolis, or can even safely claim to be on familiar terms with it. Sophie and her down-at-heel lady friends know where to get cheap eats, but that is about all: when faced with eviction and penury, they have no one to turn to. A slum lawyer named Ballot (whose name is also French slang for "nitwit") is Huysmans's portrayal of the feudalist occupation of a "receveur des rentes": someone who collected debts owed by the poor to the land-owning class. But even landowners are uneasy tenants in the shadow of a confabulated, ever-changing Paris, denoted as much by chic advertisements and brand labels as by people or markers.

For example, Huysmans creates much productive tension from Le Ponsart's return visit to Paris, where he is now nothing but an aged tourist, fumbling around, wary of spending money, tempted by prostitutes but ultimately clueless as to how to get what he wants from them. The instincts—blunted by the needs of business and economy—find themselves at a loss when confronted with the flesh, even when the flesh itself is broken down into business and economy; indeed, nothing is valued that cannot be reckoned in some currency or other. Throughout *A Dilemma*, gourmandizing, sex, and finances are densely cathected, as they are in the bourgeois mind. Money is better than sex, but sex is sometimes worth paying for; still, no sex act is as reliable as a good repast and the perfect cup of coffee (which, as every parvenu not in the know knows, can only be had at the Palais-Royal).

A nasty social comedy of manners (very ill manners), *A Dilemma* is notable for its compression and keen psychological insight. It was Huysmans's technique to push Naturalistic omniscience into an extreme terrain that verges on something well beyond ordinary realism. We see a distinctly modern perspective on the isolation of city life in the way that each character is frequently lost within his or her own thoughts, thoughts that are not communicated even to close friends and relatives: thoughts which the protagonists wish to conceal out of prudence or shame. What drives the most discursive aspects of the narrative is something that comes at the expense of his characters' frustrated attempts to bond with others or even make their own causes clearly understood: Huysmans depicts his characters only in states of relentless detachment from each other and, moreover, from themselves.

The resulting world is a desolate one: a world in which comforts are efficient and merciless, or simply not to be found, and where power is justified by a set of values whose strength depends on the hypocrisy on which they are built. Unlike the working class and the aristocracy, the bourgeoisie was a permeable, shifting body, and thus in the long run, one always ready to perceive a threat. In a dog-eat-dog world, it is swindle or be swindled: heaven helps those who help themselves. Heaven help those who cannot.

I

In the dining room, which was furnished with an earthenware furnace, cane chairs with twisted legs, and an old oak sideboard, made in Paris at Rue du Faubourg Saint-Antoine, that held behind glass panels gold-plated chafing dishes, champagne flutes, and a complete white porcelain dinner set edged with gold that had never once been used—there, beneath a photograph of Monsieur Thiers, weakly lit by a hanging ceiling light that glowed down on the tablecloth, Maître Le Ponsart and Monsieur Lambois folded their napkins, signaled with a glance for the maid to bring them coffee, and fell silent.

After the girl left, Monsieur Lambois opened a rosewood cellarette, glanced suspiciously at the door, and then, apparently reassured, spoke.

"See here, Le Ponsart, my friend," he addressed his dinner guest, "now that we're alone, let's talk a bit about what's on our minds; you're a notary; where exactly do we stand as far as the law's concerned?"

"Exactly here," the notary answered, taking a penknife with a mother-of-pearl handle out of his pocket and paring the tip of a cigar. "Your son died with no heirs; no brother, no sister, no progeny. The little he had from his late mother must, by the terms of Article 746 of the Civil Code, be divided equally between the paternal and maternal ascendants; in other words, if Jules didn't make a dent in his capital, you and I get fifty thousand francs apiece."

"Fine. But we still don't know if the poor boy had a will bequeathing a portion of his assets to a certain someone."

"Yes, that's the point that needs some clearing up."

"So," Monsieur Lambois went on, "assuming that Jules held on to all his hundred thousand francs, and died intestate, how can we get rid of that creature he was living with? And do it in such a way," he added, after a moment's thought, "that she won't attempt to blackmail us, or pay us a scandalous visit that would compromise us in this town."

"There's the rub. But I have a plan: I know how to get rid of that scamp, quietly and without much expense."

"How much do you mean by 'much expense'?"

"Heavens—a fifty at the most."

"But not the furniture?"

"Of course not the furniture . . . I'll pack that up and have it all shipped here."

"Perfect," concluded Monsieur Lambois, pulling his chair up to the stove and wincing as he stuck out his gout-swollen right foot within heating range of the furnace's open door.

Maître Le Ponsart sipped a digestif. He savored the cognac, and whistled through his lips, which he puckered like a rosette.

"My word," he said, "is this that old cognac from the uncle?"

"Yes, there's nothing like it in Paris," Monsieur Lambois stated categorically.

"Indeed!

"But look," the notary went on, "even though my position's clear, since we can't be too careful, let's review everything we know about this little missy before I leave for the capital.

"No one knows who her parents are, we don't know the circumstances under which your son fell in love with her, she possesses no education whatsoever—that is clearly evident by the grammar and penmanship of the letter she sent you and which, heeding my advice, you were right not to answer;—in short, we don't know much."

"And that's everything—I can only repeat what I've already told you; when the doctor wrote me that Jules was seriously ill, I got on the train, arrived in Paris, and found the hussy installed in my son's home and nursing him. Jules assured me that the girl worked for him as a maid. I didn't believe a single word of it, but I obeyed the orders of the doctor who told me not to upset the patient and didn't argue the matter; as the typhoid fever was growing worse with each unhappy hour, I stayed on, tolerating the presence of that phony maid to the very end. She did present herself very respectably, I have to give her that; then the removal of my poor Jules's body had to be done without delay, as you know. Busy with purchases, errands, I had no occasion to see her again, and I hadn't even heard tell of her until that letter arrived in which she declares that she's pregnant and asks me, as a favor, for a little money."

"Prelude to blackmail," the notary said, after a pause. "As women go, what's she like?"

"She's a tall, beautiful girl, a brunette with fawn-colored eyes and straight teeth; she speaks very little, and her discreet and artless demeanor leads me to think she's a crafty and dangerous person; I fear you have a tough opponent, Maître Le Ponsart."

"Bah, bah, that little hen would need strong teeth to bite an old fox like me; anyway, I still have that police commissioner friend in Paris who can help me if necessary; as crafty as she may be, I have a number of tricks up my sleeve and I'll bring her to heel if she makes any fuss; in three days my expedition will be over, and I'll come back and claim from you, as a reward for my successful endeavors, another glass of this old cognac."

"And we shall drink it with happy hearts!" cried Monsieur Lambois, momentarily forgetting his gout.

"Ah, that pea-brained boy," he went on, speaking of his son. "To think he'd never given me any trouble. He worked conscientiously at his studies, passed his exams, even lived perhaps a bit too much like a lone wolf, unsociable, no friends, no companions. Never, and I mean never, did he run up any debts, and then, all of a sudden, there he is, hooked by a woman that he fished out of who knows where. It baffles me."

"It's the way of things: children who are too precocious come to bad ends," declared the notary, standing in front of the stove and lifting the hem of his frock to warm his legs. "In fact," he continued, "the day they catch sight of a woman who strikes them as sweeter and less brazen than the rest, they think they've found the very magpie's nest, and all else be damned! The first one to come along hoodwinks them and they just don't care, even if she's silly as a goose and clumsy to boot!"

"Say what you like," replied Monsieur Lambois, "Jules was not the sort of young man to let himself be controlled that way."

"Heavens," the notary concluded philosophically, "now that we've gotten on in years, we forget how easily young men let themselves get sweet-talked by a petticoat, but if you think back to the days when we were more spry, aha, the skirts turned our heads, too. You talk, but you never gave up your share to other men, did you, my old Lambois?"

"Certainly not! Until we got married we had our fun like everyone else, but in the end, neither you nor I were ever foolish enough to fall—let's call a spade a spade—into concubinage."

"Obviously."

They grinned. The flush of their youth came back to them, leaving a bubble of saliva on Monsieur Lambois's blubbery lips and a glint in the old notary's pewter eyes; they had eaten well and drunk a vintage wine from Les Riceys, a purple-colored wine that had lost some of its alcohol content; in the warmth of the enclosed room, their heads flushed in regions long dormant, their mouths watered, excited by the entrance of that woman whom they could now ungirth, without any witnesses, at their leisure. Little by little, they worked themselves up, repeating twenty times over their tastes in women.

They only appealed to Maître Le Ponsart's senses if they were short and plump and lavishly dressed. Monsieur Lambois preferred them tall, on the thin side, and without expensive adornments; he prized refinement above all else.

"Bah! Refinement's got nothing to do with it. Parisian style, yes," said the notary with smoldering eyes; "What's most important is to not have a wooden board in bed."

And he probably would have expounded further on his sensual theories, but a cuckoo above the door, noisily chiming the hour, cut him short. "Goodness," he said, "ten o'clock! Time for me to go home if I want to be up early enough tomorrow to catch the first train." He put on his coat; the antechamber's cooler air chilled the ardor of their nostalgia. The two shook hands, uneasy now that their visions of women had evaporated, and felt their hatred grow toward that stranger with whom they intended to wage war, thinking that she was bound to hotly dispute an inheritance rightly entitled to them by the Code, that judicial monument which they revered like a tabernacle.

II

For thirty years Maître Le Ponsart had been the notary of Beauchamp, a tiny region under the Marne's jurisdiction; he had taken it over from his father, whose fortune, amassed through some transactions of a disquieting probity, had been on lazy provincial evenings endless fodder for gossip.

Before going home to the country, Maître Le Ponsart spent some time in Paris after he finished his studies, working in a lawyer's office where he was initiated into the most devious minutiae of legal procedure.

His instincts already well honed, he wasn't too stingy in spending his money up to a certain point; if, during his Paris days, he let himself squander all he had on lavish orgies, if he did not scrimp unduly with a woman, he expected to get from her in exchange a dividend of tariffed pleasures prorated to an amorous scale drawn up for his use. "Equity in all things," he would say; and as he paid out the coins in his pocket, he thought it only fair to apply a penal rate in pleasure to his money, collecting from his debtress such and such percent of caresses, but only after first deducting a carefully calculated number of considerations.

The way he saw it, only good food and girls could represent, in value, the expense they entailed; life's other pleasures were not what they promised to be, never equaling the good cheer produced by just looking at money itself, even when lying at rest in a cashbox; he thus constantly availed himself of little tricks common in the provinces, where thrift had the tenacity of leprosy; he used candle rings and push-up candlesticks so he could burn his candles down to the very ends of their wicks, and, unable to breathe coal and coke fumes without getting dizzy, he made those little "widows' hearths," in which two isolated logs glow red at a distance from each other, without warmth and flameless; roamed all over town to purchase something as cheaply as possible, and felt a keen satisfaction at the thought that others were paying more, keeping the best places a carefully guarded secret from everyone, laughing up his sleeve, proud of himself, thinking how clever he was when he saw his companions slapping each other's backs over bargains that were in no way such.

Like most provincials, he could not take out his wallet in a store without feeling uneasy; he would go in with the firm intention of buying something, meticulously examine the merchandise, decide that it suited him, knew it was cheaper and better made there than anywhere else, but at the point of making up his mind he remained hesitant, asking himself if the purchase were truly something he needed, if its merits were enough to outweigh the expense; and even more like most provincials, he never had his linen washed in Paris for fear of the laundresses scorching them, he said, with bleach; he shipped it all in crates to Beauchamp by train, because, as everyone knows, country laundresses are trustworthy, and their irons kind.

In sum, his carnal proclivities had been the only ones powerful enough to overcome, at least up to a point, his penchant for thrift; particularly wary when it was a matter of helping a friend, Maître Le Ponsart wouldn't dole out the slightest amount without weighing up the consequences; but rather than extend a hundred sous to a starving acquaintance, he preferred, if he saw no way to avoid doing the favor, to offer to buy the borrower an eight-franc dinner, so that at least he himself could partake of half the meal and draw some benefit from the expense.

His first concern, upon returning to Beauchamp after his father's death, was to marry a rich, ugly woman;

he had from her a daughter who was every bit as ugly, and sickly to boot, whom he married off at a very young age to Monsieur Lambois, then twenty-five years old and already embarking on a business career which the town described as "sizable."

A widower now, Maître Le Ponsart continued to make use of his practice, though he often felt an urge to sell it and return to live in Paris, where his deceptive employment of skilled consideration wouldn't be lost in an atmosphere both warm and lanuginous.

And yet where could he have found a more favorable, less hostile environment? He was the most respected citizen in this Beauchamp, which wasn't sparing in its admiration—an admiration that showed traces, truth be told, of respect and fear. Whenever his name was praised, as it generally was, someone would habitually let slip this qualifying statement: "All the same, it's best to stay on his good side," and the nodding heads suggested that Maître Le Ponsart was never one to let his grudges go unavenged.

His stature alone, disconcerting to all, was enough to forestall the slightest of trespasses; his watery complexion, his cheekbones streaked with pink veins, his beveled nose turned up at the tip, his white hair coiled on his nape and covering his ears, his toiling vintner's shoulders, his familiar paunch like that of a plump parish priest, had a warm-hearted brio to them that was alluring, prompting one to trust him at first and almost tap his belly cheerily, before suddenly being frozen by his tin stare, by the winter of his cold eyes.

Ultimately, no one in Beauchamp fathomed the true nature of this old man, praised above all because he seemed to represent Parisian refinement in the province, and who nonetheless never denied where he came from, remaining a pure provincial in spite of his sojourn in the capital.

To the entire town he was the supreme Parisian, for his toiletries and clothing came from Paris and he subscribed to *Parisian Life*, whose tolerated elegance made his grave eyes sparkle; but he balanced out these society tastes with a subscription to the *Moliérist*, a review in which a number of fellows toiled away elucidating hitherto unknown information concerning the life of the "Great Comic." He was even a contributor—Molière's humor being well within his ken—and his love for this indisputable glory was such that he had set about rewriting *The Bourgeois Gentleman* in verse; this prodigious labor had been in the works for seven years; he tried hard to follow the text word for word, earning great respect for this fine work, although he set it aside now and then to draft occasional poems which he delighted in reeling off on birthdays or at banquets—any intimate gathering where people rose to propose toasts.

But he was also the supreme provincial: he was interested in gossip, liked his food, and was a skinflint;

repressing his sensual urges, which he could not satisfy in such a small town without some shameful ruckus, he acknowledged the charms of good food, and hosted tasty dinners, all while cutting back on the lighting and the cigars. "A gourmet, that Maître Le Ponsart," the preceptor and the mayor would say, jealous of his parties even as they talked them up. At first, this luxurious food and subscription to an expensive Parisian journal almost exceeded the dose of Parisianism that Beauchamp was able to take; the notary nearly acquired the reputation of an old playboy and spendthrift; but soon enough, his fellow citizens recognized him as one of their own, driven by the same passions, the same hatreds; the fact is that, though keeping it a professional secret, Maître Le Ponsart encouraged slander and relished petty gossip; moreover, he so loved profit, and so praised saving, that his compatriots grew excited listening to him, stirred to their very core by these theories, which they loved enough to listen to on a daily basis, and which they found to be always poignant, always new. The subject was inexhaustible for them: here, there, everywhere, money was the only topic of conversation; no sooner was someone's name mentioned than it was immediately followed by an enumeration of his assets: those he possessed and those coming to him. These thoroughgoing countryfolk even cited dead parents, told malicious anecdotes, scrutinized how fortunes had been made, weighing them up within twenty sous.

"Ah, his great intelligence is equaled only by his great discretion!" proclaimed the elite of Beauchamp's bourgeoisie. "And such a distinguished man," the ladies added. "What a shame that his spendthrift days are behind him!" resumed the chorus, for despite the adulation that enveloped him, Maître Le Ponsart let himself be desired, acting the flirt, so as to keep his prestige intact; and yet, whenever he made occasional business trips to Paris, the citizens of Beauchamp who shared subscriptions to the *Figaro* were always a bit surprised that the paper never announced the arrival of such an important person in the metropolis, when each day, in the "Business Trips and Vacations" column, they made a point to note the departures and arrivals "within our walls" of caliphs of industry and country squires, to the keen satisfaction of the reading public, who were duly impressed, albeit quite unfamiliar with the names.

The glory that shone around Maître Le Ponsart reflected somewhat upon his son-in-law and friend, Monsieur Lambois, a former hosier who had established himself in Reims and retired to Beauchamp, his fortune made. A widower like his father-in-law and a man of leisure, Monsieur Lambois whiled away his idle hours in cantons, where he inquired about the care of livestock and the best way to grow grain; he pestered the deputies, the prefect, the subprefect, the mayor, and all the adjutants, with an eye on an election in which he wished to run for general councilman.

Joining electoral committees, poisoning the lives of the deputies he harassed, filling his pockets with letters of recommendation, always running errands, he held forth at meetings, spoke of our era hurtling into the future, maintained that the deputy, who was in the hot seat, was happy to go on nursing at the bosom of his constituency, extolled the imposing majesty of the people convening in their own comitia, described the ballot box as a peaceful weapon, even cited a few of Monsieur de Tocqueville's comments on decentralization, and debated for two hours straight, without spraying saliva, newfangled industrial technologies guaranteed to bring wealth and success.

He dreamed of serving as general councilman but had not yet been able to angle for the seat of deputy, who was wise to his scheme and had firmly resolved not to let his post be stolen from him; he had dreamed of it not only for himself, whose financial greed was already sated, but also for his son, whom he had destined for the calling of the prefecture. Once Jules would have passed his dissertation, Monsieur Lambois had very much hoped, through his patronage and his maneuvers, to get him an appointment as a subprefect, and then prefect. He even counted on having a strong enough influence with the deputies that they would place him at the head of the entire Marne jurisdiction; then it would be his very own progeny—his, Lambois, retired hosier—governing his compatriots and administering over his hometown.

Without a doubt, in the promotion of his son to such a lofty rank, he had seen a kind of honor conferred upon his family, of whose commonality he nonetheless boasted, a type of aristocracy in opposition to the genuine one, which he spat upon, even if it was with envy.

But that whole scaffold of longing had collapsed; his son's death had dimmed that vainglorious future, enshrouded that proud horizon in fog; he had reeled from the blow, and his family ambitions had crumbled into personal ones, the two becoming fused. With great bitterness, he now sought a position on the county council, and with Maître Le Ponsart guiding him step by step, he advanced little by little, without mishap, often bowing as he went, hoping that an appointment would be handed to him, with no serious rivals in the way, no steep costs to be paid. Everything had been going as planned, and now here was the threat of that harlot, rallying the entire countryside in support of a little Lambois, locked up within the temporary prison of her bulging belly!

"Jules must have told her my plans in one of his more effusive moments," he moaned on the day he received that woman's request for money.

"Ah, this is our vulnerable point, our Achilles' heel," the notary sighed after reading the missive, and in spite of the principles they paraded about, both felt nostalgic for the old days when men with motives similar to theirs could use *lettres de cachet* to have anyone at all thrown into the Bastille.

III

"One of the sweetest moments in life," growled Maître Le Ponsart, who had lunched copiously at the Boeuf à la Mode and was now ensconced in the rotunda of the Palais-Royal, the only spot where, like any good provincial, he believed he could get a decent cup of coffee. He caught his breath, lethargic, his head tilted slightly back as delicious lassitude flowed through his limbs. He was lucky: the day looked to be a good one; at nine o'clock that morning, he had gone to the office of the notary who handled his grandson's affairs; no trace of a will; from there he ran straight to the Crédit Lyonnais, which held that money whose suspected loss had been disturbing his slumber: the deposit was still there. He had been decidedly spared the most arduous part of his job; the woman, with whom he was ready to cross swords, possessed, at least as far as he could see, no legal leg to stand on.—"Ah, yes, this is all beginning quite auspiciously," he murmured, exhaling cigar smoke in little blue puffs.

Then he had one of those philosophical insights into life which occur so often to ruminative people when torpor begins to overtake them, when their hunger pangs have been stilled and their bellies filled. "It's only natural that women are so skilled at fleecing men!" he said, delighted by this unexpected reflection. The thought gradually expanded, branching out into each one of those physical attributes that give a woman her ineluctable power. He daydreamed about the main course of the rump, the dessert of the mouth, the side dishes of the breasts, fed on all of these imaginary details until they came together, blurred into a whole, into a kind of universal female, erotically naked, the whole of which roused in him this second reflection, as unoriginal as the first had been, to which it was for that matter only the needless corollary: "Even the cleverest of us get conned."

When it came to this, he knew whereof he spoke, Maître Le Ponsart, whose throbbing blood and bullish neck had not diminished with age. Past sixty, his eyesight had markedly dimmed, but his body remained virile and strong; since the death of his wife, he suffered from migraines, from bouts of congestion which his doctor hadn't hesitated to ascribe to the chronic celibacy he was forced to endure in Beauchamp.

His sixty-fifth year had come and gone, and bawdy urges still besieged him. That robust appetite which, in the days of his youth and his middle age, helped him to satisfy his hunger—more through the sheer number of dishes than their succulence—had been refined by age into the discernments of the gourmet; but here again, the provinces left their thumbprint on his taste; his craving for elegance marked him as a man far from Paris, a wealthy peasant, a parvenu who buys rhinestones, is lured by flashy tinsel, dazzled by garish velvet and big, gold-plated baubles.

As he sipped his demitasse, he now recalled how, in Beauchamp, sitting at his desk overlooking a horizon of green files, he had digested those particular refinements that haunted him, and which all came entirely from that *Parisian Life* that arrived by mail, and which he read the way one performs devotions over a breviary. It gave him a perspective on current fashions that seemed all the more desirable since his youthful days in Paris had been neither imaginative nor wealthy enough to approach anything remotely like it. Nevertheless, though he was there in person now, he hesitated to verify such opulence by taking part in it, for, despite his lustful nature, the innate avarice of his race deterred him from such purchases; he restrained himself to creating an ideal which he had agreed to believe inaccessible, to simply hope to brush up against it to whatever degree he could, under the least expensive and least humiliating of circumstances possible; for the common sense of the meticulous old man—of the notary—curbed that poetry of public places by admitting very frankly that he was past the age where he could hope to attract a woman. After the abstinence he observed in Beauchamp, Maître Le Ponsart still felt able to do justice to a meal, if it was preceded by some aperitif caresses and was laid out upon a white tablecloth, on a set of dishes still young, uncracked, unwrinkled; but he knew, also from experience, that he would inevitably find himself sitting opposite a dinner guest who only nibbled her food and to whom his appetite would communicate no craving.

These thoughts returned to him mainly because he was in Paris, alone, far from the eyes of a small town, free to do as he pleased, his wallet well lined, his head a bit warm from all that imitation Bordeaux.

He had read the latest issue of *Parisian Life*, and the whole thing enthralled him, from the sugarcoated human-interest stories and nude sketches in the opening pages to the silver-tongued advertisements.

Those giddy articles hammering home cavalry victories and the downfalls of noblewomen thrilled him, to be sure, though he had some doubts as to whether as much mischief occurred in the Saint-Germain neighborhood as they claimed: still, more than all the implausible fluff, it was the advertisements—neat, clean, set off in a box in the middle of some mendacious tale—that were ductile for dreaming. However much it smacked of that hyperbole necessary for sales purposes, he nonetheless remained astounded and tickled by the imperturbable guarantee in the announcement of a product that existed, that could be bought, a product which was not, in sum, the figment of a journalist's imagination, a ruse invented for the sake of a byline.

Therefore, even as it caused him to smile, Mamilla Milk immediately evoked the delightful spectacle of a perfectly rounded bosom; even the disbelief he felt regarding the vividly proclaimed health benefits of this concoction helped carry him off into a pleasant daydream, for he clearly read between the advertisement's lines the unofficial way of using this milk, saw the whole operation take place before his eyes, the bosom set free from the blouse and gently rubbed; and those nude, though inevitably flat breasts accelerated his fantasies all the more, swelling through successively added layers of flesh into those enormous jugs his cupped hands loved to hold.

His aged spirit, stuffed with bureaucracy, saturated with the pleasures of saving, relaxed into the imaginary bath in which she was soaking, in that magazine washroom covered in shelves of perfumes whose labels warbled the debatable hosannas of skin restored and rejuvenated, foreheads salvaged from wrinkles, and noses set free from their blackheads!

"I was definitely not cut out to be a homebody stuck in the provinces," Maître Le Ponsart sighed, dazzled by the cortege of elegant scenes parading through his mind—and he smiled, deeply flattered by this latest proof that his soul was really that of a poet;—then, associations with women led him to think of the one who was the cause of his journey.—"I'm curious to see this scatterbrain," he said; "If I'm to believe Lambois, she'll be a big, appetizing girl with fawn-colored eyes, a plump brunette; heh, heh, that would prove that Jules had had good taste." He tried to picture her, conjuring up, to the detriment of the real woman whom he must inevitably find inferior to the imagined one, a superb hussy whose burgeoning charms he itemized, trembling.

But this spiritual delight grew tedious, and he became calm again. He checked his watch: as it was not yet time to see his grandson's mistress, he asked the waiter to bring him the paper; he leafed through it disinterestedly.—She mounted a fresh attack, despotically, flattened his will to bury himself in politics, and alone remained, implanted in his mind and before his eyes.

He told himself he was being silly and shook his head, looking around the café for some distraction, then he sniffed in the air for traces of the pipes that brought the gas into the remarkable pendant lamps suspended from the ceiling, coated like the meerschaum of an old pipe; killed time by counting the spoons arranged in a fan, in a beaker of German silver on the countertop; to give his games some variety, he looked out the windows at the sprawling park, nearly deserted at this hour, with its handful of flaking statues, its multicolored kiosks, and its pathways lined by trees with twisted, green-smudged trunks; in the distance a tiny fountain rose out of a basin like the feather from a colonel's helmet: the whole thing looked like one of those dioramas always reeking of evergreen and paste, like some faded New Year's toy, squeezed, like a big box of dominos with the lid off, between the four walls formed by identical houses.

This scene quickly bored him; his attention returned to the interior of the café: it, too, was a little emptier; two strangers were smoking, three gentlemen were hiding behind open newspapers, showing only hands on the paper and feet emerging from trousers underneath the tables; a waiter was yawning on a chair, a tea towel on his shoulder, and the hostess was balancing the books. The place gave off the vaguely musty stench of the Restoration mingled with Louis-Philippe, which was to Maître Le Ponsart's liking. The ghost of the old National Guard, in bearskin cap and white knee-breeches, seemed to return to this round, glass-sided armoire, where foreigners and provincials who came out of habit to quench their thirst would never leave a single wisp of themselves, not a trace. All the same, he decided to leave; the weather was cold and dry; his obsessive thoughts evaporated; the notary now headed to the man's home, the quarrel regaining the upper hand now that he had digested fully; he walked faster.

"It's possible she won't be home," he murmured. "But it's better to catch her by surprise; her defenses are probably down; I have a better chance of breaking her by making a sneak attack, out of nowhere."

He trotted along the sidewalks, checking the enameled name plates, afraid of getting lost in this Paris he no longer knew. Somehow or other, he made it to Rue du Four, examined the street numbers, and stopped in front of a building that was new; the vestibule walls stuccoed like nougat, curtains hanging on copper rods, the banister's glass pommels, the breadth of the staircase struck him as comfortable; the concierge, seated behind wide shuttered doors, seemed presumptuous to him, harsh, like a Protestant minister in the pulpit. He twisted the door handle and his impression changed; this martinet lorded over a lodge that stank of cabbage and onions.

"Mademoiselle Sophie Mouveau?" he asked.

The concierge sized him up, and said in a voice slurred by Trois-Six brandy: "Fifth floor, down the hallway, third door on your right."

Maître Le Ponsart started to climb, grumbling about the excessive number of steps. Reaching the fifth-floor landing, he mopped his brow, got his bearings in the dark corridor, groped his way along the wall, found the third door, someone's key still stuck in the lock, and not finding a bell, rapped one little tap upon the wood with the handle of his umbrella.

The door opened. The shape of a woman emerged from the shadows. Maître Le Ponsart stepped into pitch black. He stated his name and title. Saying nothing, the woman pushed through a second door and led him into a small bedroom; there, it was no longer night, but twilight, in the middle of the day. Light descended into a courtyard that had the width of a chimney flue, sloping down, gray and dirty, into the room through an attic window that gave no view.

"Heavens," the woman said, "I haven't even straightened up!"

Maître Le Ponsart shrugged and began:

"Madame, as I have had the honor of informing you, I am Jules's grandfather; as cobeneficiary of the deceased and in the absence of Monsieur Lambois, for whom I have power of attorney, I ask your permission first of all to make an inventory of any documents left by my grandson."

The woman looked at him with an expression at once dumbfounded and plaintive.

"Well?" he asked.

"But I don't know where Jules kept his papers. He had a drawer in which he put all his letters; over there, in that table."

Maître Le Ponsart nodded, took off his gloves, which he placed on the brim of his hat, and went over to one of those small, orangeade-colored mahogany desks from which one pulls out with difficulty a sheepskin-surfaced writing board. He was already getting used to the darkness of the room, and little by little he could make out the furniture. Hanging above the desk, leaning out from the wall on a green string whose knots were hidden behind picture-hooks and a frame, was a photograph of Monsieur Thiers, similar to the one that hung in the father's dining room in Beauchamp—the statesman was obviously an object of special veneration within that family;—to the left stretched the rumpled bed with its piled-up pillows; to the right stood the fireplace whose mantle was filled with medicine bottles; behind Maître Le Ponsart, on the opposite side of the room, sagged one of those small sofa beds upholstered in that blue rep which sunlight and dust turn muddy and brown.

The woman had sat down upon this sofa bed. The notary, uncomfortable at feeling someone behind him, turned and implored her not to interrupt her domestic duties on his account, invited her to behave as if she were in her own home, giving slight emphasis to these phrases, and thus laying the groundwork for the commencement of his operations. She did not seem to grasp the meaning he was giving to his words and remained seated, silent, persistently staring at the mantle that was decorated with pharmacy phials.

"Goodness!" thought Maître Le Ponsart, "this cheeky little hussy is tough; she's afraid of compromising herself by opening her mouth." He turned his back to her, his belly before the table; he began to feel exasperated, trying to decide where to begin; given the means he presumed that this woman had adopted, he would have to dot every *i*, grope his way forward, haphazardly attack an entrenched enemy laying in wait for him. "Could she have a will in hand?" he asked himself, his temples suddenly damp with sweat.

Her outward appearance, which he had stared at when leaning over her, both worried and angered him. Impossible to decipher any thoughts whatsoever on her face; she seemed dazed and speechless; the fawn-colored eyes Monsieur Lambois had praised were empty; no precise meaning could be assigned to their gleaming.

While unwrapping the bundles of letters, Maître Le Ponsart reflected. The bit of benevolence he had been able to summon with the end of a good digestion had vanished. She was a real slattern, this girl! Shapely, if a bit too skinny for his liking, she was dressed in a gray flannel camisole with brown stripes, a blue apron, filoselle stockings, shod in old slippers with open sides and flat heels.

That instinctive indulgence he had tendered toward the woman as he had imagined her, a gorgeous hussy, plump and curvaceous, in silk stockings and satin slippers, smelling of venison and face powder, gave way to indifference, even contempt. "Dear lord, was that poor Jules green!" he said to himself, by way of conclusion. Suddenly, the thought that she was pregnant flashed across his mind.

He put on his spectacles, which the old man had hid away when he thought he was going to encounter an elegant and fleshy young lady, and he brusquely turned to face her.

It was true that her thighs did seem stocky, slightly fulsome; beneath her apron her stomach bulged; examined with greater care, her face did appear to him a bit bruised; she had obviously not lied in her letter. The woman looked at him, taken aback by how fixedly he stared at her; Maître Le Ponsart thought it time to break the silence.

"Do you have a lease?" he asked her.

"A lease?"

"Yes, did Jules sign a contract with the landlord that guarantees him, barring certain conditions, the enjoyment of this apartment for three, six, or nine years?"

"No, Monsieur, not that I know of."

"Well, so much the better."

He turned his back once again and this time began his task in earnest.

He quickly checked the letters he opened; they were all regarding trivial matters and held no allusion to that woman whose unknown background pestered him; none of the other bundles yielded him any information either; he contented himself with noting down the addresses of the correspondents should he need to consult them as a last resort; finally he examined a sheaf of paid bills set to one side; this he immediately slipped into his pocket. In sum, there was no document which could enlighten him as to the deceased's bequests; but who could say whether or not this woman hadn't already removed a will that she was waiting for the right moment to reveal? He was on pins and needles, exasperated at his grandson and at this girl; he resolved to clear up the uncertainty which delayed him from putting his plan into action, yet he hesitated to ask the question bluntly, apprehensive over showing the weak side of his hand, over admitting that he was worried, and also afraid of alerting this woman to some course of action which she might not have otherwise seriously entertained.

"Bah! In any event, it would be highly unlikely," he murmured, in response to that last objection; and he made up his mind.

"Look, my dear child," and this fatherly tone caught Sophie off guard, even as she felt chilled to the bone by the notary's taciturn gaze; "look, are you absolutely certain that our poor friend kept no other documents, for, to be completely frank with you, I'm surprised to find not a single word, not a line, which mentions leaving anything to any of his friends. Generally, when one is kindhearted—and my dear Jules certainly was!—one leaves a little gift, a bauble, a trinket . . . this knife for example, or this pincushion . . . a memento of some sort to the people who loved you. How could Jules, having had all the time in the world to settle his accounts, just die like that, selfishly, to put it plainly, without thinking of anyone else?"

He stared at the woman attentively; he saw her eyes suddenly fill with tears.

"And you, you who cared for him so devotedly, it's impossible that he would have forgotten you!" He said this in a warm, almost indignant voice.

"Never mind," he thought to himself, "I'll risk all." The tears he had glimpsed had suddenly persuaded him. "She's getting emotional; she'll own up to everything if I pressure her," he thought. And he reversed his tactic, asked the question, contrary to how he had held himself back before, frankly but softly, now almost completely certain that the woman had no will in her possession, for he couldn't imagine that she would be weeping over her lover's memory, and with no hesitation attributed her grief to regret over not having that document.

"Yes, Monsieur," she said, wiping her eyes, "when he became so ill, Jules said he wished to leave me enough to live on, but then he died before putting it down on paper."

"How inconsiderate is youth," Maître Le Ponsart pontificated gravely. And he remained silent for a moment or two, hiding the great jubilation he was feeling. His chest felt a hundred kilos lighter; his hand was flush with trumps. "Get ready for my grand slam, you, and without further delay," he thought.

He stood up, paced the room with a preoccupied air, looking down at Sophie who remained motionless, twisting her handkerchief between her fingers.

"He certainly lacked sophistication, my grandson did, for this dear girl's extremely rustic!" And he leered at her slightly thick hands, her index finger peppery from sewing, her nails dull from housework and notched from cooking. "Badly dressed, no style, a Jeanneton doll!" he thought. Without even realizing it, this observation worsened the woman's case for him. The badly combed hair that fell upon her cheeks prompted him to be brutal.

"Mademoiselle," and he stopped in front of her, "I must, nonetheless, come to the point. Monsieur Lambois, while acknowledging the good care that you provided to his son as a maid, cannot of course allow this situation to continue. I am going to give notice on the apartment this very day, for it is the 15th of the month and it is time; tomorrow I will have the furniture shipped out; all that is left is the pecuniary question concerning you.

"Monsieur Lambois reasoned, and I share his opinion, that given the hardworking qualities you have displayed, Jules could not have had any servant as devoted as you for less than forty-five francs per month, maximum, in Paris, as you are not unaware—whereas we country folk," added the notary parenthetically, "we have servants for a far more reasonable rate, but that's neither here nor there.—So, today's the 15th, that makes two weeks plus one in advance that I owe you, which is to say thirty-three francs and seventy-five centimes, if my math is correct. Just sign this receipt for that amount."

The woman stood up, alarmed.

"But Monsieur, I'm not a maid, you know perfectly well what I was to Jules; I'm pregnant, I even wrote . . ."

"Pardon me for cutting you off," said Maître Le Ponsart. "If I've understood you correctly, you were Jules's mistress. In that case, that's a whole different kettle of fish: you have no rights to anything at all."

She was dumbstruck by this slap in the face.

"So, just like that," she said, choking, "you're throwing me out without money, with the child I'm going to have."

"Not at all, mademoiselle, not at all; you're changing the subject; I am not throwing you out, only as the mistress: I'm giving you your week in advance, as a maid, which is not the same thing. Look, mark me well; you were introduced to Jules's father as a servant. You played that role for the entire duration of Monsieur Lambois's stay here. Thus, Monsieur Lambois is unaware or at least ostensibly unaware of the relations that you carried on with his son. As he is unwell right now, confined to his house with an attack of gout, he asked me to come to Paris on his behalf, to settle any pending business transactions of the estate, and obviously he has concluded that the services of a maid will no longer be required here, since the only person who could make use of them is no longer with us."

Sophie burst out sobbing.

"But I took care of him, I spent every single night with him, and I'd do it again if I had to, because he loved me. Ah, he was a kind man! He would have given up everything rather than cause me worry. No he certainly wouldn't have thrown out a woman he'd gotten pregnant!"

"Oh, we'll leave that question aside for now," the notary quickly said. "When you claim, as you are now doing, that you are pregnant by Jules, you'll agree that it is unseemly for a man of my age to probe into your intimate mysteries; I must absolutely decline to accept that task. By the way," he went on, struck by a sudden inspiration, "how many months along are you?"

"Four months, monsieur."

Maître Le Ponsart appeared to weigh the matter. "Four months! But Jules had already taken ill, therefore he must have abstained, for medical reasons, from those intimacies which only healthy persons can allow themselves. There would thus follow the presumption that it wasn't he . . ."

"But he wasn't bedridden four months ago," Sophie cried indignantly at these suppositions. "The doctor hadn't even been summoned . . . and he loved me so much and . . ."

Maître Le Ponsart held up his hand.

"Okay, okay," he said, "that's enough," and, a bit vexed at having gotten on the wrong track and failed to trip the woman up regarding the exact number of months, he tartly added: "I already suspected that excesses must have caused Jules's illness and hastened his death, now I am certain of it; when one is no stronger than that poor boy was, he was truly unlucky to stumble on someone who is . . . well, how should I say this, too healthy, too earthy," he said, very pleased with this last epithet, to his mind choice and conclusive.

Sophie stared at him, stupefied by this accusation; she didn't even have the courage to respond, so outrageous were the charges he brought against her; the idea that anyone could blame her affection for the death of that man whom she had cared for day and night appalled her; she choked, then her tears, which had seemed cried out, flowed all the more copiously.

As she did so, the notary decided her crying didn't make her any prettier: that stomach, heaving in time with her sobs, even seemed grotesque to him.

This observation did not make him feel inclined to mercy; yet, as the unfortunate woman's despair grew, for she was now crying her eyes out, her head in her hands, he did soften slightly, and admitted to himself that it might be a bit cruel to throw a woman out like that onto the streets with just a few hours' notice.

He grew irritated, vexed with himself for what he was about to do and also for the semblance of pity in his heart.

He unwittingly tried to come up with a conclusive argument that would make this girl more hateful to him, an argument that would strengthen and justify his severity, that would relieve him of the touch of disquiet he was feeling stab at him from within.

He asked two questions, but with some dishonesty so as to convince himself, and to force the woman into giving the answer he hoped to hear, he got at the truth by telling a lie.

"In short, my dear child," he said, "I am not unaware of the manner in which my grandson knew you. That certainly doesn't detract from your merits, but if you don't mind my saying so, he was not the first to deflower those delightful charms," and here he gallantly waved his hand, "so as far as that may be concerned, as we say, we men of law, since objective fact is all that matters to us, there is no compensation owed you on that account."

Sophie continued to weep softly: she said nothing.

"Good," thought Maître Le Ponsart, "she's not denying it; it looks like I've hit the nail on the head; Jules was not her first lover—one down, one to go . . . ."

"Secondly," he went on, "you understand, don't you, that the irregular arrangement in which you were living with my grandson could not have gone on. One way or another, it would have been broken off. Either Jules would have been named subprefect of some province and he would have honorably married into a wealthy family, or, for some reason which the future alone could have revealed to us, he would have left you or you would have left him: in either event, your liaison would have run its course."

"No, monsieur," she said sharply, her head raised, "no, Jules would not have abandoned me. He would have married the mother of his child; he told me that many times!"

"There we go, you little hussy," the notary muttered; "That's what I wanted you to admit." This time her scruples had taken cover; without even the excuse of losing her virginity to his grandson, this girl had nursed the prospect of marrying him!

"This takes the cake," he said to himself; "We nearly had this slattern in our family!" He remained disconcerted; in a rapid series of images he pictured Jules bringing this woman home, passing through the village, everyone at their door, coming into a family appalled by this bad match; he saw this woman, with no formal attire, with neither table manners nor good posture, changing conversation topics with no rhyme or reason, compromising his position through the ridiculousness of her present life and the disgrace of her past life. "Well, that was a close one!"

All at once, his determination was steadfast.

"Will you sign this receipt, yes or no?" he said curtly.

She shook her head.

"Heed what I'm saying: I am offering you a way out, and you are refusing it; take care that I don't close the door."

Then, when he saw that she stubbornly kept quiet, he swallowed his anger, crossed his arms, and spoke again in a fatherly tone:

"Take my advice, don't dig your heels in; first, it won't get you anywhere; think: if you refuse to sign this receipt, what will happen? You will find yourself out on the street, without a penny to your name, when it will be too late to take me up on my offer; look, in the interest of that innocent little one you're carrying there in your bowels, don't persist in rejecting this offer, which is the only one acceptable since it's the only one that satisfies the interests of both parties. Come now, do what's right . . ."

He shoved the receipt in her face.

She pushed it away. "No, I won't sign it, we will wait and see; after all, I'm going to raise his child, which is mine . . ."

"Now ask me to hold him over the baptismal font and pay for a wet nurse," said Maître Le Ponsart, almost mockingly, so baroque her claim seemed to him! "My dear, anyone can see that the father's identity is unknown and immaterial, you don't need to be a genius to know that . . . So then, can we settle this?—because I'm in a hurry! For the second and final time, I repeat: either you are Jules's maid, in which case you are entitled to the sum of thirty-three francs and seventy-five centimes; or else you are his mistress, in which case you are entitled to nothing at all; between these two prospects, choose the one which seems more advantageous to you.

"And that's a dilemma if I've ever seen one," he said as an aside, quite pleased with himself. He gathered up his umbrella and hat.

Sophie grew infuriated. "Fine, I am going to see what options I have," she cried.

"Not one, pretty lady, trust me. In the meantime, you have until noon tomorrow to think it over. After that, I'll be leaving and taking the furniture, and I shall return the key to this apartment to the landlord; may the night give you counsel; allow me to hope that you will benefit from it, and that tomorrow you will come to your senses."

And, politely, he bowed and, seeing that she wasn't moving, as if petrified, asked her ironically not to trouble herself with seeing him out, and like a well-bred man, he opened the door and closed it very quietly behind him.

IV

Perched behind the counter of her shop, Madame Champagne loved to hear the sound of her own voice. She was asthmatic and obese, pallid and puffy, with overcooked red hair. Within her flowing fabrics, wrinkles crisscrossed in every direction, striping her forehead, cracking her eyes, lacerating her cheeks; these wrinkles were etched upon her face darkly, as if the dust of time had seeped under her skin and imbued her dermis with indelible marks.

She was loquacious and rambled, convinced of her own importance, and revered by the neighborhood, which deemed her a woman of justice with considerable pull. Indeed, she was the salvation of the poor, writing up petitions which she sent to France's most illustrious names, who often responded to them, without anyone knowing why.

In contrast, her own business affairs were less than stellar; on Rue du Vieux-Colombier, near the Croix-Rouge, she ran a poorly stocked stationery shop and newsstand, earning just enough to avoid bankruptcy; but she considered herself happy all the same, for the dearest of her wishes had come true, her love for gossiping had finally been satisfied inside that store, which formed its own neighborhood Intelligence Bureau, a sort of little police headquarters where, if not sentences and crimes, at least cuckoldry and quarrels, loans made and unpaid household debts were recorded on spoken judicial registers.

There figured prominently, among the poor women whom she defended and recommended to the charity of the society ladies, one Madame Dauriatte, sixty-eight years old, skinny and stooped, her eyes glazed over, her mouth empty and sunken, with an unctuous demeanor. She bore the classic characteristics of a leech, but even more of one of those mendicants who beg for alms in church porches, and indeed that was where she spent much of her time, being on good terms with the priests of Saint-Sulpice, and living in a state of devotion allocated equally between Madame Champagne and the Virgin.

That day, Madame Dauriatte, seated on a chair in the stationery shop, was moaning about her legs which refused to support her, and about her feet, overgrown by a small garden of bunions, those large, cultivated feet of hers which required her to wear boots filled out with pouches.

Madame Champagne was nodding her head by way of sympathy when suddenly she cried out: "Look, it's Sophie! Oh my, just look at her eyes!"

"Where?" asked Madame Dauriatte, craning her neck.

The stationer didn't have time to reply; the door opened with the tinkle of a bell, and Sophie Mouveau, her eyes puffy from crying, came in and burst into tears in front of the two women.

"Come, come, what's the matter?" asked Madame Champagne.

"Don't just keep crying like that!" said Madame Dauriatte at the same time.

They bustled about her, pushed her onto a chair, forced her to drink some vulnerary diluted with water to lift her mood, and also took the opportunity to pour themselves a small glass. "Now we can hear everything," declared Madame Dauriatte, wiping her mouth with the back of her sleeve.

And so, pestered by the two women, whose eyes were sputtering with curiosity, Sophie told them everything that had happened between her and Jules's grandfather.

There was a moment of silence.

"That old rat, damn him!" cried Madame Dauriatte, using this oath to let out, like steam through a valve, the indignation built up in her elderly soul.

Madame Champagne, who had a cooler head, reflected.

"And when is he coming back?" she asked Sophie after a pause.

"Tomorrow, before noon."

Then the stationer held up a finger and uttered the following statement like an oracle: "We have no time to waste; but you can take it from me, you have nothing to worry about. You're pregnant, aren't you? Well then, the family must provide you with room and board; I'm not a genius at law but I know that much; the main thing's not to get bamboozled. Furthermore, as sure as my name's Madame Champagne, I'm going to show that old crocodile who he's dealing with!" And she stood up. "My hat, my shawl," she said to Madame Dauriatte, who was frozen in admiration. She put them on. "I'm leaving the shop in your care for a bit, my dear;—as for you, my girl, stop crying your eyes out and come along with me: we're going just down the street to see my lawyer."

Given the assurance Madame Champagne expressed in such a virile manner, Sophie fought back her tears. "He's a very good man, you see, that Monsieur Ballot," said the stationer while they walked; "that man could sweat money from a stone wall, nothing is beyond his scope, he knows everything, you'll see; here we are, let's go up, no, wait until I catch my breath."

They climbed the three floors with difficulty and came to a stop in front of a door adorned with a copper plaque on which the following inscription had been inlaid in red and black: "Ballot, Debt Collector, please turn the knob." Madame Champagne panted, leaning against the banister: "I'm just too fat, it's pathetic," she sighed; then she hurriedly exhaled, blew her nose, and, gathering herself together, opened the door as if she were entering a chapel.

They entered a dining room converted into an office, whose window was blocked by two wooden tables painted black, with men bent over them, one old, his cranium tufted with chick fuzz; the other one young, scrawny, and hairy; neither of these two employees deigned to look up.

"Is Monsieur Ballot available?" asked Madame Champagne.

"Don't know," said the old man, without moving.

"He's busy," the young one barked over his shoulder.

"Then we'll wait."

And Madame Champagne grabbed the two chairs that hadn't been offered. They sat down in silence; her eyes downcast, Sophie was unable to put two coherent thoughts together, still reeling from the blow delivered by the notary that morning; the stationer looked around the room, furnished with gray filing cabinets, boxes, folders bound with straps; it smelled of badly scraped boots, burnt fat, and dried ink; occasionally, a voice could be heard from behind a green tambour door facing the casement window.

"That's his office," Madame Champagne whispered to her protégé, whose worries didn't seem to lessen with this interesting revelation.

So the stationer went over the thoughts she was planning to express; then, to kill time, she studied the old clerk's shoes, their torn uppers, their elastics curling like worms, their warped heels; she had started to nod off when the green tambour door slid open before the businessman, who escorted a client out to the stairwell with hearty farewells, came back in and, recognizing Madame Champagne, asked her to come inside.

The two women, who had risen from their seats the moment he had appeared, followed him into his office on tiptoe; courteously, he pointed them to some chairs, tilted back in his mahogany, semicircular backed armchair, and, playing idly with an enormous, oar-shaped paper cutter, asked his clients to tell him the object of their visit.

Sophie began her story, but Madame Champagne spoke at the same time, grafting her personal observations to the already patchwork account of what transpired. Weary of this inextricable verbiage, Monsieur Ballot wished to ask questions one at a time, and beseeched Madame Champagne to refrain from speaking and allow the injured party to explain things for herself.

After hearing the full story, he asked, "And now you would like . . . ?"

"But, we want to see him brought to justice," cried the stationer, deciding it was time for her to speak again. "The poor child is pregnant by that boy; and he's dead, he can no longer do anything for her, that's obvious, but the family owes her, in my firm opinion, a little money, if only to pay for the wet-nurse and raise the kid! Because those skinflints and stone-hearts told her they'd put her out on the street tomorrow, I came here to find out what we can do."

"Not a thing, my dear lady."

"What, not a thing!" exclaimed the stationer, utterly stupefied. "You mean that the poor of this world no longer have any protection! Anyone at all can just ruin another person whenever he feels like it!"

Monsieur Ballot shrugged. "The apartment was in the name of the deceased, and the furniture too, correct? Okay; next, Monsieur Jules has heirs, well, these heirs have the right to act as they see fit in this particular case! As for this posthumous child, whom you feel has given some grounds for Mademoiselle, that is an error, pure and simple; nothing, absolutely nothing, you understand, can force them to recognize the paternity of this baby as belonging to Monsieur Jules."

"Why, in all my life!" gasped Madame Champagne.

"That's how it is; that's the Code and it's categorical," said the businessman, smiling.

"Well, that's a fine mess, your Code is! I wonder what's in it if it can't resolve a case like Sophie's!"

"But it is resolved, my dear Madame Champagne, and that's precisely why Mademoiselle is unable to lay claim to anything through legal action."

"Come, come, my girl," cried the stationer, losing her temper. She rose to her feet. "It's obvious that these laws were made by men; everything for them, nothing for us; I will personally claw out the eyes of Jules's grandfather if I catch him; consider that a promise!" And driven to the end of her rope by Monsieur Ballot's mocking laughter, Madame Champagne grew wild with rage and vowed that if a man ever tried to do anything this loathsome to her, she would take her revenge and let the chips fall where they may, even if it meant going to court; then she added further that she didn't give a damn about the police, the prisons, the judges, and she continued her rant for a good ten minutes, worked up by Monsieur Ballot who, seeing no profit to be made from this case, was amused, and felt a basic liking for that provincial notary whose clever dilemma he was able to appreciate as a connoisseur.

As for Sophie, she remained nailed in place, paralyzed, staring into space. Since that morning, the thought that she was going to wander about, penniless, homeless, thrown out in the street like a dog, had worn her down; from that sharp, precise pain there had finally issued a hazy, almost gentle grief; she was awake but asleep, incapable of fighting the languishment that cradled her. She had stopped weeping, resigned, entrusting herself to Madame Champagne, placing her destiny in her hands, losing interest even in her own self, pitying with the stationer the misery of some woman who was of great concern to her but who was no longer entirely her.

Bewildered at this debilitation, this dazed indifference, which always comes after someone has been crying for a long time, Madame Champagne grew irritated.

"Come on, move," she said, "stop sitting there like a bump on a log!" expending the last drops of her anger in this outburst; then she pulled herself together a bit and, cool-headed again, addressed the lawyer.

"So, Monsieur Ballot, is that all that you can tell us?"

"Alas, yes, my dear lady! I regret not being able to assist you in this ordeal," and he steered them politely to the door, proclaiming as he did so how devoted he was to them, and assuring Madame Champagne in particular of his high esteem.

They returned, annihilated, to the shop. Now it was Madame Dauriatte's turn to lose her temper. Madame Champagne leaned against the counter, her head in her hands, roused periodically by angry outbursts from her old friend who was, that day, particularly incoherent. From the topic of Sophie, she ended up talking about herself without any logical transition, relating the life of the late Monsieur Dauriatte, her husband, a man whose social standing she had either forgotten or never knew, for if she could recall that he wore some gold on his clothing, she couldn't say exactly whether he had been Marshal of France or a drum major, a razor-strop paste salesman or Swiss.

This spray of stories put the stationer to sleep, exhausted from the day's intense emotions; a customer haggling over some pens woke her up.

She stretched, and thought about supper; it was getting late; Madame Dauriatte was persuaded to go to the "Dix-Huit Marmites," a cheap restaurant on Rue du Dragon, near the Croix-Rouge, and get two orders of soup and two legs of lamb, for three. "I'll grind the coffee while you get the food," Madame Champagne concluded, and Sophie, meanwhile, set the table.

Twenty minutes later, they were seated in the store's backroom, furnished only with a round table, a sink, a small furnace, and three chairs.

Sophie was unable to swallow; every bite stuck in her throat.

"Come on, my dear," said Madame Dauriatte, who was eating like an ogre, "you have to force yourself a bit."

But the young woman shook her head, feeding Titi, the stationery shop's little wolfhound, the meat that was congealing on her plate.

And as Madame Dauriatte kept insisting: "Let her be, sorrow is its own nourishment," spoke Madame Champagne judiciously, who, having lost her appetite that evening as well, at least was feeding herself with some glasses of a red liquid.

Madame Dauriatte nodded in agreement but didn't breathe a word, for her cheeks were like balls, and she was in such a rush to clean her plate that rivulets of juice were snaking down to her chin.

"Let's see now," said the stationer, putting out her wood spirit lamp and pouring boiling water over the coffee, "let's see, let's get straight to the point: Sophie, what will you do tomorrow?"

The young woman shrugged forlornly.

"Perhaps we could go and see the landlord," ventured Madame Champagne, "and ask her for a few days' grace."

"Oh, those bourgeois! They always close ranks against the poor!" exclaimed Madame Dauriatte, in a confused glimmer of clear thinking.

"The fact is that the old man has surely been to see her already, so he can take the furniture away tomorrow," murmured Madame Champagne; "I wouldn't put it past him that he even paid her off to evict you. Oh, they're heartless! Well, all the same, I'd stop them from tossing me away, in spite of all their laws; no, really, I wouldn't give them the satisfaction!"

She stopped short and looked at Sophie, who was drinking her coffee sip by sip with a teaspoon, and she cried:

"Don't drink like that, my girl, it'll give you gas!"

Then she paused for a moment, thinking, trying to regain the train of thought that had been interrupted by that piece of advice; unable to get back to it: "Anyway," she resumed, "in short, what I want to say is that when there's enough for two, there's enough for three; I am penniless, my girl, but that means nothing; if they throw you out, you'll come here and you'll have a bed and some grub while you're expecting."

Suddenly a new idea germinated in her brain.

"But wait . . . since you're not very resourceful, what if I went and talked to Jules's grandfather for you; maybe by reasoning with him I can get him to give you some compensation."

Sophie eagerly agreed.

"Ah, Madame Champagne, you're so good!" she said, kissing her; "I don't know how I would have gotten through this without you."

It was a ray of light in the gloom of her distress. Knowing the stationer's keen intelligence, her excellent upbringing, she had no doubt that her presence would be a favorable precaution; she would get justice for Sophie, who freely admitted that she lacked understanding and wasn't very clever. When she had left her home, a small village near Beauvais, she knew nothing, she had been taught nothing by her father and mother except how to take their frequent beatings. Her story was as banal as it gets. Chased after by the son of a rich farmer and then immediately fired after the bloody carnage of a rape, she was then beaten half to death by her father, who was angry at her for not having been clever enough to get the young man to marry her; she had run away to Paris and found work as a nanny for a bourgeois family who let her almost starve to death.

By chance, Jules met her; he became infatuated with this beautiful young girl, who lacked formal education but demonstrated a caring personality and a certain instinct for tact. Accustomed to rebuffs, she in turn fell in love with this shy, slightly awkward young man, who pampered her instead of ordering her about; she gladly accepted his invitation to live with him. Their domestic life was one long happiness; wishing to please her lover, she made an effort to polish herself, slowly abandoned the quietude that covered over her rough speech, knew when it was appropriate to hold her tongue; while he, hating dances, cafés, and brazen girls with whom he lost all composure, was content to stay at home with a woman whose somewhat sheepish tenderness reassured him and gave him confidence; then the day came when she realized she was pregnant, and Jules bravely acknowledged the child, flattered to be taking on serious responsibilities at his age.

Out of nowhere, without anyone knowing how, the young man fell gravely ill. Then their blissful daily routine ended. On top of her anguish and worry over the illness, she was terrified by the probable arrival of Jules's father. She endeavored to postpone if not completely fend off that threat; since her lover always shipped his laundry to his father's house, she had to wear his socks and starched shirts to get them dirty before packing them up and sending them off to the country; this subterfuge had worked at first, but soon Monsieur Lambois, surprised at not receiving regular letters from his son, had complained; though sick, Jules had gathered his strength to scribble out a few lines, whose rambling uncertainty turned his father's bafflement into alarm; at the same time the doctor, determining that his patient had not long to live, felt it necessary to alert the family, and Monsieur Lambois came at once.

She had hidden in the kitchen, confining herself to a subordinate role as maid, brewing herbal tea, never breathing a word, pantomiming, in spite of the sobs that rose in her throat, the indifference of a modern servant before the dying man, whom she devoured with caresses the instant the father returned to his hotel.

And yet, as meek and simple as she was, and albeit completely unaware of the warnings the doctor had given the father, she knew perfectly well that he had not fallen for her ploys. Besides, a thousand details in the apartment gave away their life together: the spare mattress stripped from the bed and laid out on the dining room's parquet, the complete bareness of the maid's quarters, the fact that there was only one basin, the two toothbrushes in the same glass, the single jar of cold cream always on the washstand. She had taken the precaution of removing her dresses from the mirrored armoire; but she had not thought of the other clues, so disconcerted was she by the father's sudden arrival; little by little, she noticed these oversights, and clumsily tried to hide the compromising objects, not realizing that she had dispelled, through this very effort, any doubts that Monsieur Lambois may have still had.

He couldn't have been more dignified. He allowed Sophie to wait on him, and, to save money, had her cook his meals, and he even deigned to compliment some of her dishes.

He never once alluded to the role she was playing; only after his son's death did he let on that he knew the truth, when he handed Sophie a photograph of her that he had found in one of the desk's half-open drawers, telling her: "Mademoiselle, I am returning to you this portrait whose place can no longer be in this piece of furniture."—And, with the headaches of the funeral, and shipping the body to the country, he had, as it were, forgotten her, sending her neither money nor further word.

Since then, she had been living in something like a stupor, crying her eyes out for her poor Jules, sick with exhaustion and tormented by her pregnancy, living on only a few sous a day, still hoping that her lover's father would come to her aid. Then, at the end of her resources, she had written him a vivid letter, ears pricked up, hoping for a response which did not come and which only brought in its place the visit of the terrible old man who was sending her packing.

Finally, fortune was now smiling on her a bit in spite of everything; Madame Champagne, whom she had gotten to know through purchasing newspapers and ink and then coming by for a chat at the shop each morning when she went to the market, had agreed to help her. Apart from the fact that she had a quick tongue, a gift for gab, and a lot of experience, thought Sophie, she was an established woman, a shopkeeper who had actually been married. It was no longer a poor girl like herself, who could be sent packing because she was defenseless, without a respectable job, that the notary would now have to battle; leaping from one extreme to the other, from gloomy despondency to strong hope, Sophie was certain that her poverty was about to come to an end, and Madame Dauriatte, with a platitude, expressed aloud what the young woman was thinking to herself.

"It's in the bag, my child, because, you see, with folks of a certain ilk, an understanding can always be arrived at." She went on to say that they certainly must have exaggerated the threat represented by the notary, who could not really be that bad a man on account of his wealth, which she suddenly imagined, for no apparent reason, to be incalculable; and in good faith now, after rhapsodizing this notarial fortune, Madame Dauriatte expressed an immense respect for that old man whom she had deeply despised until then.

For her part, Madame Champagne could only but feel a certain pride at the idea that she would speak with this respectable gentleman, that she would converse with him as a woman of the world; this mission made her feel like a person of supreme importance. What a story to tell in the coming months! What a coup in that neighborhood, which would praise her noble heart, extol her diplomatic ingenuity, and would go on and on about her respectability! She got lost in this daydream, smiled beatifically, already rehearsing some beneficial effects of a pout on her lips for the next day.

"Is he decorated?" she suddenly asked Sophie. The young woman didn't recall seeing any red on the man's outfit. The stationer was sorry to hear it, for it would have made the meeting all the more prestigious, but she consoled herself by repeating that never in her life had such an occasion presented itself for displaying her talents and her charm.

In place of the earlier sadness, an overflow of joy now filled the shop.—"Come on, let's have a quick drink, beautiful," Madame Champagne suggested to Sophie. "And you, my dear?" she said to Madame Dauriatte. The latter didn't have to be asked twice; she held out her cup, never saying when, hoping it might get filled to the brim; but the stationer poured her no more than a thimbleful, and they clinked glasses all around, wishing each other in unison long health and good fortune.

At closing time, Sophie, feeling more comforted, almost calm after so many shocks, no longer doubted the success of the enterprise, already calculating the amount of the sum that she would be getting, and, looking ahead, divided it into parts: so much for the midwife, so much for the wet nurse, so much for herself until she found a new job.

"You should also put a little bit aside for a rainy day," Madame Champagne wisely advised, and they laughed, thinking that life was good; Titi the dog, roused by their mirth, yapped, jumped onto the table like a baby goat, and made them laugh even harder as he brushed the happy faces of the three women with the tip of his tail.

"I have an idea!" Madame Dauriatte suddenly exclaimed.

She got up, looked for an old deck of cards and began a game of patience. "You'll see, my girl, tomorrow you will be in luck; cut, no, with your left hand, because you're not married."—And she drew three cards and, seeing that two of them belonged to the same suit, kept them and turned over the one that was closer to her thumb.

"You're the Queen of Clubs, you see, because you're a brunette, and the Queen of Spades is a brunette, too, but she can only be a widow or a wicked woman; which wouldn't be true for you."

She went through the thirty-two cards three times, discarding some into her skirt with each draw; seventeen cards remained on the table, the necessary odd number; and now she counted with her fingers, going from right to left, starting with her heroine, the Queen of Clubs; "one, two, three, four, five," stopping at this last card. "The nine of clubs!" she cried triumphantly, "that means money. One, two, three, four, five, given by this King, a reliable man. One, two, three, four, five . . ."

"Six, pick up sticks. Seven, eight, lay them straight!" added Madame Champagne.

But engrossed in her cards, Madame Dauriatte did not deign to acknowledge this childish interruption.

"Five!" she went on, "a nine of diamonds, that means papers, right next to this King of Clubs, who's a lawyer. That's it! You can rest easy, your fate is good."

"And tomorrow's another day," barked Madame Champagne, who gathered all the cards with one sweep of her hand, "so let's get some sleep, for we need to get up early!" She squeezed the hand of Madame Dauriatte, who promised to take her place as soon as the shop was open, and kissing Sophie on both cheeks, she encouraged her to straighten up the apartment, get dressed and all dolled up first thing in the morning. She herself, as excited as if it were the eve of a holiday, thought she'd put on all her jewels and wear her fancy dress again, to make herself equal to the task at hand and impress this notary, who would surely be flattered to find such company waiting to receive him.

V

At his age! To get conned by a whore solicited at Chez
Peters! Maître Le Ponsart regretted his mistake, that inexplicable push, that irrational drive that had, as it were,
compelled him to buy the woman drinks and see her
home.

Yet his head had been clear, unclouded by any wine;
that hussy had just come over and sat down at his table,
chatting him up about this and that, even though he
had warned her in all honesty that she was wasting her
time; then some gentlemen had come in and greeted her,
to whom she had held out her hand and spoken softly.
Perhaps it was this insignificant detail that spurred deep
within him an instinctive determination to have her;
perhaps it all came down to a question of etiquette, the
stubbornness of a man who had been there first and

wants to keep his place, a certain annoyance at finding himself in competition with younger men, a certain older man's pride in being propositioned by a tart, even if he had to pay too much, almost a preference—but no, none of that was true; there had been an irresistible impulse, a machination beyond his control, for he had not been set on any carnal desire and that woman was not his physical type in any way, shape, or form; moreover, the weather was chilly and dry, so Maître Le Ponsart could not even blame his helpless lethargy on the influence of those humid days or steamy, rain-streaked skies that make a man listless, easy prey for any woman on the prowl. All things considered, that adventure remained incomprehensible.

In the cab on the way there, he told himself how ridiculous he was being, that this encounter was silly, likely to be a swindle or a disappointment; still he felt utterly powerless to leave that girl he was following automatically, drawn by that strange spell known to stragglers in the evening, which no psychology has managed to explain.

He had even twisted the blade in his wound, repeating over and over: "If anyone saw me! I look like an old lecher!"—murmuring, as he paid the driver and the woman was ringing at her door: "Here's where it gets boring; she'll offer to hold my hand so I don't break my neck in the dark on the stairs, and then, once inside her room, the begging will begin! Good Lord! How stupid can I be!"—Yet he went up all the same and everything happened exactly as he knew it would.

He nevertheless received a certain compensation for the chagrin he had conceived in advance. The apartment was furnished with a luxury whose bad taste escaped him. The mantlepiece, draped in curtains of fake brocade, the andirons with pommels shaped like fleurs-de-lis, the brass clock and wall lamps fitted with pink candles bent from the heat, the divans upholstered in crocheted guipure, the thuya and rosewood furnishings, the bed standing in the middle of the bedroom, the console tables bedecked with imitation Dresden china grotesques, the trade-fair glassware, and the Grévin statuettes all struck him as betraying an appetizing elegance and a languid comfort. He stared bemusedly at the clock's unmoving pendulum as the woman took off her hat.

She turned to him and talked business.

The notary winced, dribbling out louis one by one, which the practitioner extirpated from him through a patient medley of ingratiating and imperious demands, consoling himself a bit for his weakness at being an old man sitting late in life in a whore's room with the view of her bodice, which he judged to be firm and warm, and the red silk stockings which seemed to him to crackle, in the glimmers of the candles, over plump calves and firm thighs.

To speed up the harvesting of his purse, the woman planted herself on his lap.

"I'm heavy, aren't I?"

Though his legs buckled, he politely maintained the opposite, trying his best to persuade himself, moreover, to keep his spirits up, that her heaviness could only be attributed to the solid, ample curves he had glimpsed, but more than the prospect of being able to handle them later, at his leisure, it was the calculation of his expenditures, the reasoned observation of his stupidity, and his inexplicable inability to extricate himself from the situation that overcame him and turned him cold.

With that, the woman became insatiable; with the questionable guarantee of ideal caresses, she again insisted that he add another louis to those he had already handed over. Even her inane chatter, her pet names like "my big darling," "my sweetie pie," "my little hubby," managed to fill the numb old man with consternation, and his presence of mind doubted the veracity of that promise which accompanied the requisitions: "Come on, just do it, I'll be very nice, you'll be happy."

Weary of the battle, convinced that the impending pleasures she was forecasting would be mediocre at best, he passionately hoped that they would get it over with so he could make his escape.

This desire ended up overcoming his resistance and he allowed her to completely rob him.

Then she invited him to hang up his overcoat and make himself comfortable. She herself began to undress, taking off those articles of clothing that could get crumpled. He went over to her, but alas!—that portliness that had unsettled him a bit was at once artificial and mushy!—And she aggravated this final disillusionment with all the bad grace a woman can bring to bed, claiming to be uninterested in his preferences, pushing his head away, grumbling: "No, leave me alone, you're getting on my nerves"; then, despite her being who she was, pulling a curt, disdainful pout: "You were quite mistaken if you thought I was *that* kind of woman."

He let out a sigh of relief as he made his way to the door. He had been well and truly fleeced! And his face flushed as the whole miserable scene flashed through his mind.

Then that money, extorted from him, choked him. He started thinking of all the useful things he could have obtained with that same sum.

He pondered over that fruitless observation that swindled people make: how we deprive ourselves of buying something useful or pleasant in order to save money, yet we don't hesitate to spend the same amount on something stupid and fruitless.

"Ah, you! . . . You'd better watch your step," he concluded, thinking of his grandson's mistress, applying the same reproach to the two women.

Yet he smiled, for he was sure of keeping Sophie Mouveau in check, of making reprisals against her with impunity, of taking revenge on her for all the tribulations inflicted by the cupidity of her sex. The landlord, delighted to come back into immediate possession of his apartment, had—after having, moreover, as a family man, expressed a few impromptu thoughts on the pitfalls of vice and the profound corruption of the times—proven to be well disposed in supporting the notary in his undertakings, and the concierge was respectfully inclined, when Maître Le Ponsart had shown her the order allowing for the furniture to be moved out, to assist, if need be, in evicting the woman and keeping the key; a pair of hundred-sou coins slipped into her palm had even softened her expression and relaxed the Lutheran rigidity of her bearing. "Thirty-three francs seventy-five plus ten francs make forty-three seventy-five," thought the notary; "that's indeed the number I quoted to dear old Lambois, a fifty at most."

He had taken every precaution: the movers were to show up at the door at noon sharp, carry the furniture downstairs, and send it by train, carriage and all, set flat without wheels, on a cargo truck all the way to Beauchamp.

One question remained: Sophie seemed unusually wily to Maître Le Ponsart. The silence which she nearly always observed and her way of crying nonstop disconcerted the notary, who attributed the girl's total helplessness and stupidity to shrewdness. He was absolutely convinced that her lachrymose stupor concealed an ambush of some kind, and the fear that she would yet show up in Beauchamp to cause a scandal through her very presence never left him. After some deliberation, he had made up his mind to resort to the good offices of his old friend the Police Commissioner, and through him was recommended to his colleague in the sixth arrondissement, who had promised to threaten the woman with criminal charges if she refused to keep quiet.

"Time to finish this game and send that little missy packing," thought Maître Le Ponsart, checking his watch. And he walked up to Rue du Four, consoling himself for his troubles with the thought that he would get on the train that evening and finally return to his bedroom slippers.

The concierge nearly kissed his feet, so deeply did she bow when he appeared. Maître Le Ponsart climbed the stairs, stopped at the landing, and, without even thinking about it, naturally forwent the polite discreet knock he had given yesterday for a sharp and imperious rap.

He was surprised, when he entered the room, to discover a large lady behind Sophie.

This lady stood up, gave a slight bow, and then sat back down. "What is the meaning of this?" he asked himself, looking at that paunchy woman fit to burst in a dress of hideous ultramarine, upon whose neckline fell three layers of buttery chin.

Seeing the pink coral pearls dangling from her crimson earlobes and a Jeannette cross twitching under the to-and-fro of an oceanic bosom, he thought the old lady was a fishwife dressed in her holiday clothes.

Very contemptuously, he turned his head and trained his eyes on the young woman; then he frowned. She, too, was dressed up, bedecked with all the jewelry that Jules had given her, and, dolled up like that, her breasts well defined by her blouse, her hips hugged snugly by her cashmere skirt, she was charming. Unfortunately for her, her beauty and her attire, which would have probably swayed the old man the day before, only served to irritate him today because they reminded him of his previous evening's disaster. It was bad luck; Sophie's slovenly appearance, which had repelled him on his first visit, was the only one that could have mollified him today.

Just as the stray hairs matted to her forehead made him brutal toward her at their first meeting, so now her meticulously combed hair brought out his cruelty.

He asked her harshly if she had decided to sign his receipt.

"Heavens, Monsieur!" said the large lady, intervening. "Allow me to appeal to your kind heart; as you see, the poor child is completely dumbfounded by what is happening to her . . . She doesn't know . . . I assured her that you would not let her down like this in her distress. Sophie, I told her, Monsieur Ponsart is an educated man; with people like that, who have a sense of justice, you have nothing to fear. Eh? Tell him, isn't that what I said?"

"Pardon me, Madame," said the notary, "but I would be pleased to know whom I have the honor of addressing."

The large lady stood and bowed.

"I am Madame Champagne, I own the stationery shop at number 4. My late husband, Monsieur Champagne . . ."

Maître Le Ponsart cut her off with a wave and said very curtly:

"I take it that you are related to Mademoiselle?"

"No, Monsieur, but I may as well be; I am like a mother to her."

"Then, Madame, allow me to inform you that this matter doesn't concern you; I will therefore continue to deal with Mademoiselle alone." He took out his watch. "In five minutes the movers will be here, and I will only leave this apartment, I assure you, with the key in my pocket. Consequently, I must, Mademoiselle, ask you to pack your belongings and let me know once and for all whether or not you accept the proposition I've put to you."

"Oh Monsieur, never in all my life!" gasped Madame Champagne.

Maître Le Ponsart fixed her with his pewter eyes and she lost the small portion of confidence that she had. Moreover, the lady, usually so outspoken and bold, seemed to be at a loss that morning, and lacking in audacity.

And indeed, one of those irreparable misfortunes, which seem almost purposefully to strike the impoverished at the worst possible moments, had befallen her when she woke up that morning.

Madame Champagne had two false teeth in the front of her upper jaw, which she took out each night and placed in a glass of water. That morning, she had carelessly taken the scrap of dentures from the water and placed it on her nightstand's marble top, where Titi the dog had snapped it up, doubtlessly thinking that it was a bone.

The stationer nearly fainted when she saw the vulcanite, the fake ivory, the fasteners, the whole apparatus get ground up. Since then, she had been keeping a tight lip for fear of revealing the gaps in her jaw, talking only by sputtering out the side of her mouth, devastated that she didn't have the money to fill in the holes. This obsessive concern, combined with a fear of showing the notary the hollowed-out spaces in her gums, paralyzed her faculties and turned her into an idiot.

The old man's terseness, his imperious tone, the contempt he continued to hold for her in spite of the trouble she had taken to look nice, turned her cold, all the more so in that she had not doubted for a moment that they would find a sympathetic reception, a friendly discussion, a whirlwind of reciprocal courtesies.

"You understood me, right?" added Maître Le Ponsart, addressing the stupefied Sophie.

She burst into sobs, and Madame Champagne, overwhelmed, forgot about her teeth and rushed to the young woman's side, kissing her and commiserating with tears of her own.

This outburst set the notary on edge; but suddenly he broke into a triumphant grin: the boots of the cart drivers were shaking the stairs outside. A fist pounded on the door like a drum roll.

The notary opened the door; the movers, already drunk, filled the rooms.

"Hey," said one, "that dame's passing out."

"I'll say, looks like she's in the family way," said another, noticing her stomach, and he went over, with a merry look in his eye, to take Sophie in his arms, as she had collapsed onto a chair.

Madame Champagne waved the pandours away.

"Water! Water!" she cried, panic-stricken, turning about.

"Don't bother about them, just get to work," said Maître Le Ponsart to the men; "I'll take care of Mademoiselle; and no funny business, is that clear?" He walked, exasperated, over to the stationer, whose arm he nervously kneaded; "Let's go, sort out her things and make it quick, or I'll pack it all up myself right now."

And he took down the skirts and camisoles hanging on the coat peg and tossed them into a corner as Madame Champagne, weeping, was massaging the young woman's temples.

The latter came to, and then, while the men were carrying away the furniture under the watchful eye of the notary, who was overseeing their descent down the stairs, Madame Champagne, realizing that the game was lost, tried to play her last card.

"Monsieur," she said, joining Maître Le Ponsart on the landing, "a word, please."

"Very well, then."

"Monsieur, since you have no pity for Sophie, who killed herself taking care of your grandson," she said in a hushed, pleading voice, "let me at least try to appeal to your spirit of justice. If you wish, as you put it, to think of Sophie as a maid, then consider that she did not take any wages for as long as she was with Monsieur Jules, and pay her for the months that she spent with him, so she can have the baby with a midwife and hire a wet nurse."

The notary started; then a mocking smile wrinkled his lips.

"Madame," he said with a ceremonious wave, "I'm deeply sorry not to be able to grant this request you've made of me; and the reason, my goodness, is very simple: you'd never get anyone to believe that a maid would remain in a house where her master didn't pay her. Thus, it is clear that Mademoiselle, to my mind, and by the very fact that she did not leave her position, must have indisputably received her earnings every month; I would add that no one asks a maid for receipts, and consequently, because there are no receipts in question, one cannot infer that Mademoiselle remains a creditor to Monsieur

Jules's estate. I return, then, and for the last time, Madame, as I'm beginning to grow tired of saying the same thing over and over again, to inviting Mademoiselle Sophie to settle her affairs and sign, notwithstanding the conditions I've stipulated, the present receipt. In exchange, I will pay her the sum to which I freely admit she has every right."

"But it's a crime, Monsieur, a disgrace, outright robbery," cried Madame Champagne, beside herself.

Maître Le Ponsart pivoted and turned his back to her, without even deigning to reply to these verbal assaults.

"As for you, leave me alone," he said on the landing to the movers, who were trying to wangle another bottle out of him; and he went inside the apartment again, brow knitted, hands behind his back.

He was in the grip of a vague rage; the stationer's intrusion into this affair in which, according to him, she had no reason to interfere, had made him want to conclude his business all the faster, so keen was his desire to vacate this Paris, which since the previous day had become unbearable to him, and return home as quickly as possible by the night train. Besides, he was determined not to exceed that maximum of fifty francs he had set for Monsieur Lambois; for him it was a point of honor to deliver on his promises, to demonstrate yet again how precise a man he was when it came to financial matters; this savings also seemed to him just compensation for his reckless spending the evening before; women can look after themselves, after all! Finally, the rapaciousness of the movers had outraged him; each one of them wanted to lay into his wallet; well, no one would get at it and no one would get anything! These motives, piling up in his mind and strengthening each other, made him insensible to all the pleading and tirades of Madame Champagne who, as soon as Maître Le Ponsart came back into the room, lost all composure and, no longer worried about undermining a case already decided on, began to make threats.

"Yes, Monsieur, yes," she said, whistling through her teeth, "I myself will come to your town, even if I have to walk the whole way, and I will turn everything upside down, do you hear me!—I'll bring the baby, I'll tell everyone whose baby it is; I'll say that you didn't even have the heart to bring this baby into the world . . ."

"Tut, tut, tut," interrupted the notary who opened his wallet, "I had foreseen this. Here is a summons from the Police Commissioner requesting Mademoiselle to appear before him; one more word and I'll use this, and I promise that Mademoiselle will keep quiet if she wants to remain at her liberty in Paris; as for you, my dear lady, I will also have you summoned by this magistrate who will bring you into line, I assure you, if you continue to talk nonsense. By all means, come to Beauchamp if your heart tells you to; I'll see to it personally that you're put behind bars, and fast . . ."

"Oh, the villain! He's vicious!" murmured Madame Champagne, who saw, horrified, rows of dark dungeons, rats, black bread, and Latude's pitcher, the whole awful backdrop of melodrama.

Satisfied by his little theatrical touch, Maître Le Ponsart went down into the courtyard, where they were loading the last pieces of furniture; then, when everything was in order, he asked the concierge to follow him and climbed back up the four flights.

"Aha! We've finally decided," he said, seeing Madame Champagne dunk a pen into an inkwell and hand it to Sophie.

And while the two women steadied each other's shaking hands to scrawl a vague signature at the bottom of the page, Maître Le Ponsart signaled to the concierge to tie up the woman's scattered things, and then clutched and pocketed the receipt on which Sophie had declared that she had served as maid in the home of Monsieur Jules Lambois, affirmed that she had received her wages in full, and attested that she was owed nothing further.

"You'll have a hard time blackmailing us after this," he thought, and he set on the mantel the sum he had been holding in ready cash since the day before.

"And now, Mesdames, I am at your disposal. And you, if you wouldn't mind removing those suitcases to the courtyard . . ." he went on, addressing the concierge.

"No, Monsieur, no, don't think you'll get away with it," moaned Madame Champagne, shaking her head as she held the half-fainting Sophie up by the arm and led her away. "You have everything that belongs to you?" and she lifted the lid of a basket which the young woman had herself filled.

The other nodded and, slowly, they made their way downstairs.

"Phew! What a hassle!" exclaimed Maître Le Ponsart, alone now, master of the apartment. He lit a cigar which his gallantry had prevented him from smoking before, so as not to bother the ladies, and he scanned the bare walls; then, out of a habit for cleanliness, with the toe of his boot he pushed into the hearth some scraps of old rags and papers that were laying on the floor; a note, folded in four, caught his attention; he picked it up and looked it over; it was a prescription from the pharmacy: distilled cherry-laurel water and tincture of nox vomica. He thought for a moment, and vaguely recalled from his experience as a married family man that this potion helped ward off nausea in pregnant women.

"Goodness!" he thought. "That girl might need this prescription!"—He opened the window that looked over the courtyard, waited for the two women to finish making their way downstairs and come into view, and then coughed loudly; when they looked up, he tossed them the scrap of paper, which fluttered down and landed at their feet.

"I don't want anything to feel guilty about!" he concluded, puffing on his cigar. He inspected the premises one last time, assured himself that they were decidedly empty, and then carefully closed the door and left in turn, returning the key to the concierge.

VI

A week after Maître Le Ponsart had returned to Beauchamp, Monsieur Lambois was pacing in his living room, consulting the clock with a worried look.

"Finally!" he said when the doorbell rang, and he rushed into the entrance hall where, calmer than ever, the notary was hanging up his jacket on the head of a stag.

"All right then, let's see, what is it?" he said, following Monsieur Lambois into the living room where a game of whist had been set up.

"I received a letter from Paris, about that girl!"

"That's all?" said Maître Le Ponsart, puckering his lips disdainfully; "I thought it was something more serious."

This assurance visibly relieved Monsieur Lambois.

"Let's read this letter before the others get here," the notary went on, giving a quick glance at the four chairs arranged symmetrically around the table.

He put on his glasses, sat down by one of the candles on the table, and attempted to decipher some lines scribbled on very glazed paper in very faint, watery ink, which bled in spots.

MONSIEUR,

I dare to take the liberty of writing to your good heart, begging that you might please to take part in my situation. Since Monsieur Ponsart came and took away the furniture, Sophie, who no longer had a place to lay her head, was taken into my home, as the child of the house; and she kept her dignity about it, Monsieur, because of her good heart, even though Monsieur Ponsart did not render unto her the justice she believed, but everybody cannot be louis d'or and please everyone . . .

"Some style!" exclaimed the notary. "But let's skip over this pointless verbiage and get to the point. Ah, here we go!"

Sophie had a very unfortunate miscarriage; she was in the back of the shop where I keep my things so that the shop in which people enter is always clean, when she was taken by pains; Madame Dauriatte . . .

"Who's this Madame Dauriatte?" asked Monsieur Lambois.

The notary shrugged to indicate that the lady's name was unknown to him, and continued:

Madame Dauriatte did not believe at first that it was going to be a miscarriage; she thought the blow of having been cast out by Monsieur Ponsart had given her bad humors, and she went to the herbalist to get some elder bark to burn and have Sophie breathe the fumes, so as to steam off the water that she must have had in her head. But the pains were in her belly and she was suffering so much that she screamed herself hoarse; at that, I was seized with fear and I ran to Rue des Canettes to a midwife whom I brought back and who said it was a miscarriage. She asked if she had fallen down or if she had drunk any absinthe or wormwood; I told her no, but she had been in great pain . . .

"Get to the point! Let's skip this babble," said Monsieur Lambois impatiently; "we won't finish before our friends arrive, and there's no point in filling them in on this whole stupid matter."

Monsieur Le Ponsart skipped ahead a page and went on:

—She died, just like that, and the child fared no better; so, as I had pawned my cross necklace and my earrings, I paid the pharmacist and the midwife, but I have no more

money and neither does Madame Dauriatte, because she never has any.

Therefore, I am begging you on both knees, my dear Monsieur, not to abandon me, I beg of you to not let her be buried in a mass grave like a stray dog. Monsieur Jules who loved her so much would weep if he only knew; I beg of you, send me the money to bury her.

Counting on your generosity . . .

"And so forth and so on," said the notary, "and it's signed: The Widow Champagne."

Monsieur Lambois and Maître Le Ponsart looked at each other; then, without saying a word, the notary shrugged, went to the fireplace, stoked the flames, placed Madame Champagne's letter in the grip of the tongs and calmly watched it burn.

"Done, so we'll have no repercussions," he said, standing back up and putting the tongs back in place.

"The three cents that stamp cost were certainly wasted," remarked Monsieur Lambois, as his father-in-law's calmness had managed to reassure him.

"Well," Maître Le Ponsart resumed, "her death brings the discussion to a close." And with an indulgent tone, he added:

"In all good conscience, we can't be angry at the poor girl anymore, despite all the headaches she gave us."

"No, certainly not, no one would wish for the death of a sinner." And, after a silence, Monsieur Lambois insinuated: "Nevertheless, you have to admit that our benevolence toward her memory is perhaps sullied by selfishness, because, in the end, if we no longer have anything to fear from that girl, who is to say whether, had she lived, she wouldn't have sunk her claws into another wealthy young man or stirred up trouble in some household?"

"Oh, no question," replied Maître Le Ponsart, "that woman's death isn't completely regrettable; but you know, unfortunately for respectable folks, there'll always be another one; plenty of fish in the sea . . ."

"Plenty of fish," echoed Monsieur Lambois, and he finished this funeral oration with a sad nod.

NOTES

p. 1, *Monsieur Thiers*: Adolphe Thiers (1797–1877), who comes up twice in this short novel, was the most powerful French politician of his time, a statesman who rose to become the first president of the Third Republic (1871–1877). Thiers was a lifelong conservative infamous for using military power to put down any attempts at working-class revolution in France, including the Commune of 1870.

p. 31, *Jeanneton doll*: This was nineteenth-century French slang for a woman who was not curvaceous but flat in the front and back: "*N'avoir ni cul ni tetons, comme la poupée de Jeanneton.*" By itself, "Jeanneton" was slang for a woman of easy virtue who worked in a bistro or an inn.

p. 72, *Latude's pitcher*: Huysmans is making a facetious reference to Jean-Henri Latude (1725–1805), one of the more bizarre criminal cases of pre-Revolution France. Latude had concocted a plan to gain favor with Madame de La Pompadour by sending her an anonymous letter filled with poison and then saving her life by revealing his knowledge of the attack before she opened it. His guilt came to light, and when he was placed in the Bastille, his shirt was covered with messages that he had scrawled in his own blood. He defied authorities in a series of bold but always unsuccessful attempts at escape, and was moved around to a number of other prisons including Vincennes and Bicêtre. He published his *Memoirs*, an account of deplorable conditions inside French prisons, which apparently impressed Marie Antoinette enough to get Louis XVI to grant him full pardon and a gentleman's pension. Latude died a wealthy celebrity in 1805.

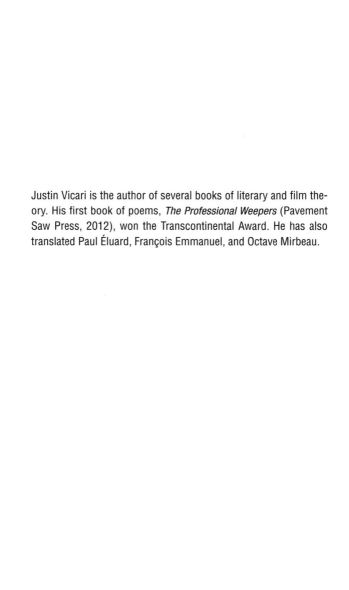

Justin Vicari is the author of several books of literary and film theory. His first book of poems, *The Professional Weepers* (Pavement Saw Press, 2012), won the Transcontinental Award. He has also translated Paul Éluard, François Emmanuel, and Octave Mirbeau.